Voices from the Society
(Vol. 2)

Compiled & Edited By
Sweta Kumari

Published by InkQuills Publishing House
www.inkquills.in

First Edition 2020

ISBN: 978-81-945636-0-0

PREFACE

This volume is in continuation to book *Voices from the Society*. It touches upon the social issues that has been left apart to reflect in this volume in form of poems, articles and stories. It deals with human suffering, women's condition and their voices against the patriarchal structure. Besides, it also focuses on the issues like casteism, gender discrimination, rape survivors, suicide, discrimination at educational level, the problem of an old age, child labour, widow's problem, smart phone addiction, acid-attack, poverty, depression and more about women's cause. Being compiler and editor of this book anthology, I do believe that the writings included in *VOICES FROM THE SOCIETY,* Vol-II will make you acquainted with different writers dealing with different existing issues that need to be eradicated from the society.

Compiler & Editor

SWETA KUMARI

DISCLAIMER

I have tried my best to check for plagiarism in the write-ups of all the contributing co-authors to this book. However, if something has escaped from my eye and if plagiarism is found later on, I shall not be liable for the same.

As I have asked all the co-authors to submit their original and unpublished works, and our bond and relationship is based on utmost good faith with them.

SWETA KUMARI

ACKNOWLEDGEMENT

First and foremost, my parents deserve special mention for supporting me all the way going ahead academically and morally. Therefore, I would like to thanks my parents to keep inspiring me a lot throughout my life. I extend hearty thanks no other than my own eldest sister, Shilpa who is always kind enough and always motivates me being my reader whatever I write. Though I am lucky enough to have her as not only my sister but also my class fellow and friend. I express my heartfelt thanks to my youngest sister, Shivani and my youngest only brother, Sourav who have always been with me in time of my need. Now, I am thankful to my Supervisor, Dr. Neeraj Kumar for his constant guidance in my academic life. I am deeply indebted to Dr. Deen Dayal for recognising my worth and motivating me to go ahead with my writing career. I am also highly grateful to Dr. Dinesh Gupta for his valuable guidance in life.

I would like to thank all my readers, admirers, all the members of my family and friends. Especially, my Facebook friends, though I don't know some in person, however they have been very positive and encouraging with their kind, inspiring and loving words. I would like to thank all my contributors to make this book anthology successful. So, I express my sincere gratitude to all of them for giving their valuable time for it.

Last but not the least; I thank all the team members and InkQuills Publishing House for giving me this opportunity to work. Since this is my first book anthology, I with their kind support, I could accomplish well. I know my words are not enough however I thank you all again for making my dream comes true for this anthology.

SWETA KUMARI

COMPILER & EDITOR

Sweta Kumari (Gold Medallist, M.A. in English) is currently a research scholar at the Department of English at Magadh University, an academician at the Literati Council Publication Division, India and an editorial member, the Global Literati Journal. Besides, she is a poetess and short story writer from Bihar, India. She has written everything from poetry, quotes and short stories to micro tales and open letters. Her writings are mostly inspired by her own life and experiences and what she herself witnessed in the society. Writing helps her lot to survive in her worst times; it is her escape from reality. After struggling between her academics and passion, she now finds solace in only and only words. She got her first two poems entitled "Tranquillity in Life" and "The Dejected House" published in an Annual Magazine of SPARC (Society for Promotion of Arts & Culture), Karim City College, Jamshedpur, 2016-17. Thus, she has contributed her writings national and international anthologies and in Journals as well. Besides social issues, her writings are focused on nature, patriotism, love and general themes. Her profile has been selected for being one of the wonderful Women in Overseas Coffee Table Book entitled 25 Wonderful Women of Virtue. Moreover, she has worked on a joint poetry project entitled A Date with Poetry in 2019 contributing her 20 poems published from Artson

Publishing House along with three other writers belonging from different states. Sweta has tried her ink to show the power to make a change through her words in this project as her poems here are mainly concerned about social issues, nature and women's cause.

She has been awarded "Father Day Presentation 2019 Best Budding Poet of The Year" and has received a certificate for Outstanding Performance Poetry Recitation Award by the Literati Council, India in an International Conference on Widow's Problem and Their Solutions. Not only that, she has been recognised with several awards for her writings in Universal Achiever Book of Record, Future Kalam's Book of Record and Honorary Degree of Doctorate, Rashtriya Ratna Award 2019, Literoma Achiever Award 2019, 2nd National Iconic Personality Award, India Star Passion Award, Uttar Pradesh Ratna Shaman 2019 and many others. She has even presented her several scholarly papers in national and international Conferences/seminars and participated actively in workshops. Her research papers are widely published reputed national and international journals and in the edited books as well. She is very much activity in her academic activities. With all these achievements, she aims to continue expressing her feelings and ideas through words, because that's what describes her best. You can connect with her:

Instagram at @sweta5259,

Facebook- Sweta Kumai

Twitter- Sweta Kumari.

CO-AUTHORS

Adegoke Tolulope Victoria

My name is Adegoke Tolulope Victoria, I was born on the 12th of April, 1999 in Ibadan, Oyo State, Nigeria. I completed my secondary school education at Oluyoro Girls Grammar School, Ibadan by 2015 and gained admission to study English by 2018. I am currently a student in the department of English in the University of Ilorin, Nigeria.)

THE PAINFUL PLEASURE

The painful pleasure of a posh society
Is to secretly satisfy a sour desire
And leave a lasting lash on the victim

An occurrence of rigour in victimization
An emblem that deprive one's happiness
An experience that leaves behind a dark memory

Escape is not sure through strong self determination
Except the adversaries chose to free you
And repent of their destructive lust

Let the workers of such iniquity be informed
That nemesis awaits them
Except they curb the selfishness of a mere wish

Then, we can become siblings
Born of a different mother
Nurtured by the same feed of integrity
And have a common goal of hope.

Arshi Anjum

Arshi Anjum lives in Lucknow Uttar Pradesh. I am a girl who is a keen devotee of Islam. I love my family a lot and follows every tradition respectfully. I am currently facing many problems but I had learnt to be strong and fighting them. I know God is always with me. I write always love poems; Love is a best creation of nature on this earth so it always keeping in my mind how such a beautiful thing like love is corrupted. I learnt to live my life as accordingly my own rules. I want to be a famous by my name as an honourable authoress or poetess like a respectable citizen in my community or society. This Article is based on life visions massages, realistic views and eternal flames.

To all lovers across the world. We thanks to all my readers. We humbly thanks to Almighty God. God has given a chance to win this opportunity. They gave a sense to know, to understand, to thank, to read and then write well thoughts through the words................!!!!

LIFE: A REAL RETOUCH

One day I was passing through near my home side then I had seen an old man and woman. They were sitting in a bench. Their facial emotions show that they were depressed. At that time, I was just passing in front of them. You know that time I realized that they wanted to say something but I was in a hurry. So, I went away from there without hearing them but their eyes were still chasing at sight. What was that moment, I really didn't know? But one thing that I really felt that they were waiting to their loving ones. In other words, we can say that they needed care and attention especially trustworthy love affection. So, this story is reality based as one day we'll be in the same situation, definitely old stage as like our loving parents. So, why we do unjust behaviour with our parents and our life partner. How disgusting why people do with their parents. We are such a selfish person. In fact, day by day, we are leading to misbehaving temper.

Parents are special gift of God. Every step of life they always push up us, follow us, cheer up us, as well they defeat every problem, which can affect you. They just always want their children to be superior in all respect. They want their children to reach the top of success. But the fact is that when the children grew up, they forget all things, all childhood memories, all games, all advices.

So, stop avoiding your parent's innocent feelings and please try to understand your parents and their emotions. They had grown old and their whole life, they have spent for you to fulfil your dreams. In another word compatibility is a word if men and women understand, the meaning of this world, any house will not be broken for the relationship.

Sometimes if you analyse people's actions, you will come to conclude that they all seek happiness. Every act is, in fact, a search for happiness, even if on the surface it doesn't look. So, going to the movies, eating in a restaurant, going to a party, traveling abroad, buying clothes or gadgets are seriously motivated by the desire to be happy. In fact, there is always this happiness factor inside you, as well as moving you to seek happiness. Some people go to the extreme with their search for happiness and likely they seek danger and take risk themselves because these acts brings them a sense of exhilarations, is a motivating factor.

Actually, no doubt we are spiritual beings in physical bodies. The spiritual part is always happy because our daily life fully depends on it. i.e. daily life can be made easier or happier. In spite of this, life is beautiful but not always so easy, it has problems too. According to a critic, "Thus life is and should not be just of bed of roses: thorns are also a part of it and should be accepted by us just as we accept the beautiful side of life. Thorns always teaches how to succeed in our life..."

At last few words for expressing whole extract. Experiences says skills are better with words, people are having very angry and aggressive attitudes. Life is too short and going to passing. The thing doesn't last as everything are sure to change.

Make sure all of you will cheer with your life with lifelong retouch amusement.

Bhawna Vishal

Mrs Bhawna Vishal, a lady born in month of October on 20/1981, from a small district Hanumangarh, Rajasthan. She loves nature, deeply believe in humanity and trust. She completed her school life from LBS, Jodhpur, she has done a diploma in electrical engineering, she accomplished her Master's in English literature, Geography and computer science. Now she's serving as a Government Senior Teacher for English. She's a writer, a teacher, speaker and as well as a house maker. she started writing at early school days and has taken part in so many speech and debate competition. Poetry for her is a way to express her feelings and also a medium to express the ongoing of society. She also loves to write shayari, stories and articles.

THAT LILY WAS NOT THERE

Lots of lilies, there were,

With sweet fragrances,

And beautiful colours,

Blossomed to shine,

She was a pinkish one,

So pure and divine,

But to her,

Fate was not kind,

The day was unfair,

The mercy was blind,

She was grabbed and crumbled,

Crushed like clay,

For society's ruthless hunger,

She was an easy prey,

Suddenly the sky became fierce,

Poisonous became the air,

And to the orchards sorrow,

That lily was not there.

AND DEPRESSION WAS DIAGNOSED

Not dumb by birth,

But taught to be,

Encaged in dead and rotten rituals,

Slave of others, she was not free,

Told to keep her scars a secret,

Not able to tell her fears,

Not allowed to express herself,

She was trained to hide her tears,

No right was available to her,

To ask for help,

To demand a justice,

But gradually her untold fears, desires,

Her scars, her suppressed inner fires,

Congested her breaths,

And paralyzed her bliss,

Then one day, she faint, she fell,

To the dark deep hell,

Finally came a help,

Her pain was exposed,

And depression was diagnosed.

Chandrima Saha

Chandrima Saha, is a resident of Guwahati, Assam. As people know Assam is one of the emerging North Eastern state known for its tourism, culture and tradition. She belongs from this state and from a family of five members. She has completed her graduation in Geology, a multidisciplinary subject of earth science. Later on, she worked as a Ground staff and gained knowledge of the work environment. She appeared for a number of competitive exams and currently she is searching for new opportunities. Addressing social issues has been one of her interests after observing the suffering of innocent people around. She communicates the same through her writings. Deep thinking about life, issues and surroundings has made her express more fluently in the writing platform. She has a YouTube channel where she shares her experiences and try to communicate with people through the related topics. She thinks every single individual has his/her own creativities, hobbies and skills. People should keep practicing it and learn more new skills with time. Failure is definitely a depression, but at the end we must recollect whatever we have learnt from the bitter experience and move on.

THE UNSPOKEN REALITIES OF CASTE RESERVATION

In a developing country like India, career and education is given utmost importance. But the path to reach there remains blur and blocked due to the Caste Reservation System. This system introduced years earlier for preserving the rights of underprivileged communities in India is still prevalent today. The age-old concept of untouchability and discrimination still being practiced today in the form of Caste Reservation.

In this modern era where it is often spoken about equality in all spheres whether it's race, religion and gender. Then why that equality is not reflected when it comes to caste? Why still the reservation system is taken intro criteria for government jobs and education? When people have stepped out of the ancient mentality of untouchability and discrimination, then why through the Caste Reservation System, that expired mentality is still being recharged?

The system of reservation introduced by the Indian Government is a major drawback in the education system today. The unreserved or the General category students have to go through a lot of struggle. Also, the reserved categories including the Scheduled Caste and Schedule tribe get a surficial benefit with only relaxation of marks and fees. However, their seat matrix remains less. Even if a reserved category candidate tops an exam, he/she is still entitled the reservation scheme instead of putting them in the merit category.

The General category students definitely have to pay a higher fee and score an unbeatable mark for getting admission in recognised educational institutions. The same goes for the government jobs too which demands extremely higher marks from the unreserved category. Nonetheless, the fee of filling up the forms for admission to government educational institutes is also high when it comes to General category. The popular entrance examinations like the management, bank and engineering ones charge ten times more fee from the General category. They appear for the exam, score sufficient marks but they stay behind and fail to realize their dreams as reservation comes into play.

There are many instances and many people around who don't even apply for a government institute or a government job observing the reservation system. Some admits that "We are from General Category and we won't get chance here if we don't score exceedingly higher." While there are also some who thinks that "We are from reserved category, but our seat matrix in this particular government vacancy is very less. We won't get here." This kind of discouragement and disappointment is cultivated in the minds of youth today.

Doesn't it sound a clear injustice? Being from the unreserved category doesn't mean that they are all equally rich. Similarly, being from the reserved category doesn't mean that they are all equally poor. But this simple logic is not clear to the authorities giving way to this blunder of reservation.

Recently, the Government has introduced the EWS category for the economically backward students from the General Category. But this is mere helpful as only one or two candidates gets this privilege based on high marks and the rest suffers.

Another unnoticeable drawback of the reservation system is that it puts a limit to the potential of reserved category students. Depending on their caste, maximum of the students doesn't show up their real forte. They become convinced to understand that their reserved caste will act as their saviour in educational and government job field.

Here I'm sharing my own story. I graduated in 2018. My reservation says I'm from OBC NCL Category. For acquiring admission in my preferred universities, I used my reservation. But I paid the form fill up charges equally as the General. Because OBC and General Category are considered the same on earning terms as per the reservation myth. However, OBC has fewer numbers of seats compared to General and a very little difference of cut off marks. I used my reservation in the fear that if I don't make to this particular university, I will face disappointments. And yes, the later only happened. Scoring one mark less than the cut off ruined my expectations. I realized at that time, if I'm depressed this pathetically, then what about those General Category students who have higher score than me but still they lost the opportunity. What about those reserved category students from SC and ST who even after claiming their scheduled status, didn't make up to their goals.

The growing children in schools today will face this caste issues later. Looking at the system, they may also use reservation as a tool for getting admission in their preferred colleges. Though, they have read about equality throughout their secondary study span, but they will be compelled to dwell in a world contrast to it. For instance, a student who is much capable but still fears that "If I don't use my caste reservation certificate, maybe I won't be able to make it."

If the Government really feels a need to spread educational and job facilities to the underprivileged sections of the society, then it should raise awareness camps and empower them to step forward and participate equally to gain a good future. I think such kind of empowerment will really give a way to the genius mind in them.

It is a serious need of the time to abolish this Caste Reservation System as it neither benefits the reserved as well as the unreserved. It is just drawing a thick margin of discrimination between people dividing them on the basis of their caste. For admission to educational institutions, only merit-based system should be practiced instead of Caste. Allowing admission on the basis of merit will not only bring pure talent in the educational field but will also encourage students to equally participate for achieving their goals in life. The cut off marks laid by universities and colleges must be equal for all without establishing a bridge between.

Also, for government jobs only genuine talent should be appreciated and taken into account for employment. There should not be any barrier like Caste Reservation and related issue.

"Free the country today from these blunders and let pure capability do the wonders."

Chinmay Divyadarshi

Chinmay Divyadarshi Kar, the Author is a 21-year-old student currently pursuing his Final year MBBS in Institute of Medical Sciences and SUM hospital under Siksha 'O' Anusandhan (SOA) University, Bhubaneswar. In the hectic Medical Curriculum, he discovered his interest in Literature and Poetry. Being newly gifted with his skills of writing, he aspires to make his best self to come out to reflect upon his career. He also holds interest on the mysteries of the human brain function and its response on various changes occurring in our day to day lives and hence is also drawn towards the field of medical research and Rare medical case seminars. He believes on a day when every human in planet would understand the true value of emotions. During his 2nd year of MBBS, he wrote and published his book named *CATHARSIS: A TALE OF IMPERFECT COINCIDENCES* – A unique book containing the story of the Imperfect coincidences faced by a Medical graduate in 24 hours and his inner feelings and launched it in various popular social media platforms. After that till now he has successfully co-authored various published poetic anthologies which are now available in various social platform.

DEDICATED TO ALL THE RAPE SURVIORS AND THE LOST LOVE

There is a dance of asynchrony

Sudden rise of beats almost in monotony

Then a wave of slow beats ending in harmony

Her heart pleads for testimony

But she won't say

Here she is respiring after a traumatic event

Lungs sending an impetus of cheyne stokes respiration

She is under a spell of emotional juggernaut

Confused and angry inside but in outside scared and whimpering of some sort

Losing control little by little over her bodily function

She feels shattered, broken into a million pieces

Under the twilight street, recalling the same event she freezes

But she won't say

Her eyes are dilated, looks dehydrated

With a powerless pace and desolated face

She looks herself in the mirror and feels disgraced

Her charming smile with a gloomy frown, its replaced

She bleeds from all her orifices

But she won't say

Her world is turned upside down

Left in the world to get judged by other clowns

Burning in that same oil over and over again

Until when boredom silences the pain

But she won't say

Once a girl with vibes of Fearless red was now stained with pale yellow

Once a girl firm and robust is now left fragile and broken

Once a girl untied and unbound now felt taken and imprisoned

But she finally made herself seek help

After all she indeed said

Because she was the Hannah of 13 reasons why

She finally made every one pay

Still couldn't confess her love to her crush, A boy named Clay

But what happens to other million Hannah's

Who slit their wrist and embrace it as a proud moment of escape,

Maybe this world doesn't deserve these Hannah's

Because there aren't many much Clay's left.

BROKEN THOUGHTS

Shallow breath and dim lights

I closed my eyes when I lost that will to fight

Gazing at those dark coloured drapes

Falling down every minute in my semiconscious state

One step closer to death. One last pain to suffer

At last, Heaven be the place where I feel happy and be safer

A while later even death stabbed me in the back

They said I have done a crime from which I can't snapback

Life is a precious gift of god, His favourite piece of rock

And we the humans have no right to make it mock

For I am doomed for eternal pain

Neither heaven nor hell, it's the total silence which I gain

Watching for eternity, those 11 days after my death

Watching how everyone cried over my flesh in their fumbled breath

Watching those familiar faces who mourned for me

Watching those friendly faces who had never cared for me

Watching the parents who were a bit hard on my manner

Watching the same parents shedding tears in the corner

Watching the sibling with whom every time I fought

Watching the same sibling reading my secret diary and crying over my broken

thoughts

And after watching all these endlessly

Eyes getting filled with blood tears constantly

Only one thought comes in mind.

Was it worth it?

As quoted always …

Suicide doesn't prevent the pain. It passes it on to someone else

Dr. Savita Vardhaman Patil

Dr Savita Vardhaman Patil works as head of English department in Rayat Shikshan Sanstha's Dr Babasaheb Ambedkar College Aundh, Pune. She is a creative writer and her many poems are published in international and national magazines. She has been teaching literature to UG classes for 17 years. She has presented research papers at international and national seminars.

SECOND INNING

It is a mid-time of summer season. Leena prepares herself to go to court. Today, she is much passive as she will be getting gift of interminable solitariness legally as she was used to have earlier. Yes, Leena had engulfed with solitude in her mind but now it will be appearing on paper also; authentically, with stamp of separation. She looks at Kavya and wipes her forehead full of drops. Her situation is like budding candidate appearing for an interview, and like young girl who scares to meet her would-be-husband. Her mind is mixture of all expected; unexpected emotions. Here, she knows her future and immediately the apprehension enhances from bottom of her mind. Her interior trauma is innumerable. With borrowing courage, she smiles at Kavya; and he too reciprocates with same act. The whole room wears the silence as if the trees clad dry leaves. She stares at Kavya and drowns in glimpses of his birth.

It was a long time back; Girish was beside her in hospital. He lifted infant in his hand and played with baby. Yes, baby too was elated to see Girish's face as if both had long time bonding with each other. Girish glanced at Leena and said "Leena, thank you for this wonderful gift." He caressed her forehead. "I will be always grateful to you."

Leena said, "I'm too delighted and thankful to you for fulfilling my life with such joy."

Girish accentuated, "Leena, we will call him Kavya."

Receiving such sudden jerk, Leena's face became pale as she was in love with some fabulous names. But recalling his fascination for poetry, she kept mum. He noticed her sudden silence and uttered, "Doesn't you like it?" But borrowing some energy on body and soul; she replied. "No. no. actually not so. Its nice name." She accepted that name bit reluctantly and started to love it.

"Mumma, -- hey--where are you...?" she retains Kavya's words, hurriedly hides her humid eyes tactfully and says, "Let's go; otherwise we will be late." She murmurs in her own mind "already everything is late."

"Mumma, did you say something" says Kavya.

"No, dear nothing. Move now." replies Leena.

She remembers how reluctantly she had accepted each decision of Girish in her life, how she started to love it later. She peeps in mirror and smiles sarcastically to her words, and hastens towards the car.

She arrives in court-room and notices Girish already had been there. As usual, she glances at him. His eyes appear reddish and lids too heavy. "It seems that he too has undergone insomnia." she murmurs with such care so as her words should not blast in air. "Then what's wrong between us?" she thinks for a moment. By exhaling long sigh, she thinks that everything is useless to contemplate now; at least at this stage. Both look at each other, but surprisingly the glances are devoid of anger, hatred, envy, grudges and love also perhaps...both are doubtful.

The court room is silent as if dried river bed in summer. She usually dislikes such ghastly silence. As usual, she reluctantly adjusts with the atmosphere and closes the eyes. Yes, now, she likes this solitariness because her ship of memories sails on life-sea mutely without any external hindrances. The series of pictures starts to pass over her eye-sight. She remembers the incident of her wedding with Girish, their conversation, his likings and yes; their court-marriage also. She still recollects how Girish was obsessed with the thought of court marriage and her refusal to that idea. She had dreamt of grand celebration of their marriage. But again, she approved the proposal of court marriage. Superfluously, all was appearing goody-goody. She murmurs the word 'goody-goody' in her own mind again and again. She realizes a heavy hand on her shoulder and immediately lands on real world by the announcement in court room. She resumes the consciousness from her trance, and looks here and there. With perplexed attitude, her eyes travel in that court room. She notices the same old walls with torn pieces of colours, spider's web, and broken chairs also. Everything appears usual. She glances at Girish; he is engrossed in cell-phone. She sarcastically laughs to herself. Now, she is confident about herself in court-room. Nothing unusual; Girish usually clings to mobile. In despondent mood, she exhales a long sigh, takes out water-bottle, and drinks rapidly as if thirsty for years to years. The drops ooze from the both side of mouth. She tries to resettle in the chair and her sight goes one by one on every article in the room. She resembles her silence with every article in that room. What else can she do sit in that room? Suddenly, she attracts towards a spider that is waiting for prey, by adopting silence, without knowing anyone. At the same time, an insect slightly gets trapped in web.

"Oh, no" Leena murmurs in her mind. "What an unfortunate creature it is!"

An insect attempts to get rid of coiled web around it. But more it starts to move, the more it gets trapped tightly. After noticing this, an insect ceases to move and surrenders to the situation passively. To avoid the bitter end, Leena purposely turns her attention somewhere.

Now, she waits for "their" call in court-room. She stumbles on the word "their" still feeling alliance of relation. She suddenly looks at her crossed legs. She tries to release it. All of sudden, she senses the vibration of legs from other side. "It is Girish's legs" she whispers. Within a fraction of second, she realizes his act of listening music. Leena's guessing is right. Girish has inserted headphones in his ear to listen songs. "Music; especially classical music is his life" she says in mind by recalling past events.

Now, the strings of Leena's heart, lose in memories, begins to play. She remembers how Girirsh was fond of classical music. He usually loved to talk about Kishori Aamonkar, Pt. Bhimsen Joshi, Pt. Jasraj and all. Once, he had asked Leena about it. Leena never had had an interest in music. Once Girish said "Leena, I had never ever thought of wife like you!"

Leena uttered, "Oh! Was it so? She laughed sarcastically."

Girish noticed her audacity and said, "Leena, I really meant it."

You are always engross in kitchen and domestic work. You don't pay heed to my words."

But Leena didn't realize the seriousness of those words. She chuckled, "Well then, who will look after our home, house hold duties, Kavya and his studies. You don't take any initiative in such things so I have to...that's it.

She discarded the issue and went in kitchen. She even didn't notice his silence. Girish came nearer to her "You never take me serious."

Leena replied, "Girish, you know, I've completed commerce graduation and desired to do job. Even, I had received offers also. But you refuted the idea adhering probable dereliction towards home, Isn't it?"

Girish kept mum. Without anticipating his answer, she continued, "Even, I never express any grudges regarding. But I'm not much interested in music as like you."

Girish was speechless. She panted his cheeks mischievously and went to do her rest work.

Leena recalls how unwillingly she had accepted his decision. When Kavya began to attend higher secondary school, she started to take tuitions of accountancy at home. Now, her world was in her threshold. She disliked launching home tuitions. But leisure obliged her to do so. The classes were her mere time investment.

Kavya arrives in court-room. He looks both at them and notices silence all over. He smiles at Baba. By turning to Leena, he puts his hand on her shoulder. Leena feels very much comfortable. She blinks the eyes in content. Nobody intervenes ghostly silence. Rather, everybody adopts reticence, but engross in conversation with their inner 'selves'.

Sitting in court-room, Girish too recalls the memories of the decision of shifting of Leena and Kavya to Sangli for

Kavya's education. After completing XIIth, Kavya received admission for engineering in government college. One day, they sat together after completing dinner.

Kavya said, "Baba, I wish to pursue my engineering at Sangli."

Leena uttered. "That's fine dear. But for that you have to shift to hostel. Beta, you are not accustomed to do your own work like your Baba."

Girish's face was frowned. Leena noticing this and continued, "I mean, Kavya how will you manage this?"

Kavya replied, "Please, don't worry for that Mom, I'll manage everything."

Both turned their faces to each other. Immediately, Girish whispered, "Why don't you accompany him there, Leena?"

First time, Leena elated at his words but disapproved the proposal by adhering Girish's living needs. Now, she did not want to leave him alone. She used to worry about his sensitivity towards everything.

She said, "Girish, I know you don't need me at all. You are depended upon me only because I do work for you. And if I settle there, you will be accustomed to live without me." Upon her words, Girish expressed anger and said "a very bad joke." She said, "Oh dear! I was just kidding." Who knew that that would really come true" murmured Girish.

These words dance in Girish's ears now. He remembers how he had joined Leena and Kavya at weekends frequently. He had purchased a flat in Leena's name. He used to visit them in earlier times. Later, the visits became less and less. In court room, all these three members knit the web of their memories, errors. Kavya also reminds the day when he obtained the 'offer-letter' from the company in Hyderabad. He stared at the letter and was delighted. He was anxious to show it to parents. It was the moment of celebration for him. He handed over the letter to parents. He had taken decision to shift to Hyderabad. At the same time, Girish also had declared his determination of separation from Leena. It was like lightening fell on both.

Kavya wipes his humid eyes. Each one is lost in their own world. But they are interlinked with each other through memories.

Leena reminds how she had overheard words of Girish while talking to friends about spouse's mis-match in his life. "Oh! Were its true words then?" She blames herself for the ignorance towards all these incidents. Leena reminds the day when she received the divorce notice from Girish. She was nearly to fell down. It was a great blow to her. She had never dreamt of such day. She had suppressed a sob, thought lot, memorized too lot but didn't find the answer of the question, "Why this happened?"

She comes in consciousness. She is still haunted with the same question. The tears ooze from her eyes unknowingly. Leena takes out handkerchief, wipes her eyes. Lawyers arrive. They point out the place to sign the paper. Wiping the noses trills, Leena fumbles in purse for pen. In baffled situation, she does not get it. Her fingers search for the pen. Still, her palm remains empty. Girish offers his pen to her. But Leena politely denies accepting the pen. Then, Kavya lends his own pen to her. With trembling hand, she holds the paper. All the words appear watery to her. Her forehead is full of perspiration. The same situation she had undergone while signing the paper at the time of court marriage. With humid eyes and shuddering hands, she signs the paper. She murmurs, “my circle is completed now.” Kavya understands her words, but Leena utters, “Kavya, let’s move. I’m ready.” She immediately turns her back, walks steadily towards the gate. Girish stares at her back image silently.

Geetanshi Muttreja

Geetanshi Muttreja, an avid reader turned writer, born on June7, 1999 is a computer science student and a published writer who has earned numerous feathers in her cap. She has made her mark in the world of poetry by contributing to many poetry groups and winning prestigious awards for her excellence in literature contests. Alongside poetry, she immensely enjoys acting and has performed various dramatics one of which is *Pride and Prejudice*. Her other interests include singing, dancing, swimming and sketching. She firmly believes that poetry is the food for soul. It isn't just some words on a paper but vivid emotions written down to be enjoyed by many. Poetry writing for her is a deep passion and her poetries depict realities in life coupled with spirituality in love and Longings.

SCHOOL

Lingers my soul in a cold stairwell,

Of a closed down school more like a hellhole,

School, a dreaded place.

Where all good ideas go to waste.

Where I was pushed and my life ended,

But I don't recall having anyone offended.

Why? The question I ask myself every day.

They say 'Here all will soar',

But they forget so many will hit the floor

It's been so long; my body was left to decay.

Here I still stay,

No choice no says,

All good ideas are tossed.

Students of vision got lost.

I'm trapped in this nothingness,

All alone, nothing but a deserted space,

Painted in black and gray,

Shrouded in curtains of dust,

Carpeted with steps showing rust.

SOCIETY

Welcome to my society

A concentration of colourful tribes

Where black and white are yet another vibe

Where souls are trained

Just to have your brains drained

Welcome to my society

Where mind's only goal

Is manipulated to simply fit inside the hole

This is my society that shatters you from inside

Yet expects you to smile

Its obnoxious phenomenon of being rich

Is simply proportional to the word ditch

This is my society that stabs your happiness

And sprinkle on your wounds with little by little amount of sadness

Welcome to my society

Where teenagers are subjected to depression

And then questioned for being stressed with tension

This is my society, a dreaded place

Where all good ideas go to waste

Creativity is thrown in trash

And development seems to hit a major backlash.

Hazira Tabaz

Hazira Tabaz is the Indian women author of The Plight of my life, published in 2019. Her book was awarded for being one of India's top 100 debut authors. Her content has been published in the several landmark anthologies. She is an accomplished teacher at a prestigious school, where she has been recognized for her dedication to the advancement, education and mentorship of India's future. She strives to free her mind; her passion is to learn something innovative every day, and lives each day like there is no tomorrow. She would like to show her profound gratitude for the experiences that she has gained in her life period. Get to know more about her in all social media 😍 Hazira Tabaz.

VOICE OF A GIRL

Some says it's like this,

Few says it's like that,

But nobody says

Let her be the way she likes!

They cursed me for being a girl

Not even knew what was wrong being a girl

I was searching for my rights

No wonder that being a human

Is what made them all insane

Justice was absolutely not fair

Flawled criticism was the fare

All the boon of a girl was bane,

Her fame of beauty was only in name,

Her soul was fighting like a flame

Still the crooked society making her blame

Oh lord help out the poor girl, don't extinguish the flame.

ORDEAL OF WOMANHOOD

My parents said what will the society will think of me?!

If they see me being a girl,

As I grew up they made me criticize being what I am

Don't do this, don't do that,

No matter what the girl will feel,

If blood relationship speaks ill about a girl,

Imagine how crooked the society is?

And the girl is shamed to say where she belongs,

Either she is lost or found;

Nobody is going to hound.

Carve something profound,

Which is gonna make a good sound.

Do everything with few bounds,

Nothing is ever sound.

Care about everybody around,

Which will never be a wound.

Be yourself with mound of love,

Neither it is lost or disbound!

Keerthi

This is Keerthi from Hyderabad. I've been co-author in wild flowers rising and also compiled *Into the woods of Ramé*. I'm a graduate and ink my mind for peace and relating the world!

Instagram @_keyru_b

CROSS HER HURDLES

She wanted to make herself Strong
Strengthened enough that
Not a curse, not a hurdle
Could break her will.

She wanted to conquer her
Greatest fears
not to be called as a queen
But to be the conqueror.

All she wished was time
To get to her goal
But they say a good path
Chosen is never easy.

Yet the she tried ignoring
Those unwanted scribblings
That people drew on her soul
As she desired to be pure.

A JUST LIVING

We're just living a life,
For the sake of living,
Clueless of what we're doing,
And what's happening!!

Breathing every new day,
Not bothered around,
Just sitting rather than,
Finding a new way!!

We're hypnotized by the,
Ideals we create for ourselves,
Walking path of theirs,
Ending up to a place nowhere!

Muskan Shah

Muskan Shah, Simple girl with big dreams hails from Jharsuguda a small town in Odisha. Completed her schooling from DAV and is pursuing Course of Company Secretary currently. She has a Professional degree of an Interior Designer. Writing was not a profession but somehow became passion for her and now she is a part of 12+ Anthologies as a Co-author and have compiled an Anthology named 'Ishq Happened Again' and 'Bachpan ke Emotions' and some are in process. She really never thought to be a writer or to write, but somehow her life made her to write and Now she is following it with much Interest and Passion.

She has her YouTube channel Named 'Muskan Shah'.

Instagram Handle - The_Unpublished.Ink

DISCRIMINATION AT EDUCATIONAL LEVEL

The little small kid

Always wanted to be a doctor

Dreamt of a happy life

Just some cars and not helicopter

He wanted to be successful

And a big man with all life necessities

Unaware of the fact that the high society has signed rich to be richer treaty

His little heart always wanted to hold high

His little hand always wanted a beautiful tie

No one knew that the intelligent boy

Because of poverty has to cry

Direct discrimination on basis of

Gender, Caste, Race, Religious Belief and Age

It felt like a little bird

Kept and tortured in a cage

Right to education is a Right for all

You can't take it away because of your so-called rules

Every child in India deserve to be literate

And you can't stop them from it because of Indian society double standards mates.

Parasuraman. P

Parasuraman. P is a reader, writer, poet, listener and questioner from Tamil Nadu. He has completed his higher secondary school education, in Government higher school at Rajanthangal. He stayed and studied in hostel for 10 years. Now he is studying in BSc Visual Communication (Multi Media) at PUCC - Pondicherry University Community College. He has good professors in his college, they treat him like a friend, and also guide him the right way.

He is a God denier. Ambedkar, Periyar, follower of the principles of rationalists like Karl Marx.

Blog-parasulalitha.blogspot.com

Instagram- @parasulalitha

Twitter- @parasuraman.p

TOWARDS DOWN

Some fall and many live

It is the freedom that is acquired

There is a tall man here

There are those who are oppressed without reason

Insoluble in time

We have the shore

In spite of the appearance of vandalism

We pass as if not seen

If anthropomorphic

Respect people - here

Neither is mankind

There is no respect

Home for the vote only

The voters are just that

We are not customers

History aborigines

Wake up - our

To weed out those who hid the way

We are rushing

Join the young man - Um

Suffering away — yours

Dry the wretch to wipe

Tonight's over ...

Let the dawn of tomorrow be for you ....

THERE IS NO NEED OF WAR

Any country not defeated

will not fail

Nobody wants war

As long as nothing happens

The seeds of the sky will be rushed to the sky

The world asks for the role of soil

You're in the mood

The border of dispersion

Despite that the feeling of division

Terrorism itself will be prevented and we will avoid it.

The world appeared somewhere

Somehow going on

What do we humans have in common?

Pooja Trivedi Raval

I am Pooja Trivedi Raval. My pen name is SMIT. I know about 16 languages. I like to train people for the same. I love to evolve the ocean of my feelings on paper with a pen.

THE CHILD LABOUR AND THEIR CHILDHOOD

The most relaxed phase of life,

The most beautiful charm of the life...

However, the society wants to ask you,

The child labour is enchanted too?

Why the child is not safe?

Why the child is everywhere unsafe?

Why?

If the child goes to school

He is overburdened

He may be abused

He may be tortured

He may be punished

He is depressed

He is afraid of score

He is under pressure of show off

If he goes for labour

He is overburdened too

He is punished

He is over pressured.

He is stressed for starve

He is afraid of begging

He is stressed to be insulted...

Why?

Why not childhood can free?

All the children play on a tree?

Don't they need love?

Why he can be burnt by stove?

Only to save from child labour is enough?

Don't you think after saving his life we made it tough?

Who is responsible for it?

Why they are not getting twice a day to eat?

Don't you think society is for all?

Everyone is responsible for the fall?

Stand up, take a stand

They don't need money they need your hand.

WOMEN EMPOWERMENT

What is women empowerment?

Or It should be women enlightenment?

What is actually needed?

Don't you think women empowerment is seeded?

Women empowerment is

To have hold for the food cooked in the kitchen

To have hold on budgeting

To have hold to take off hands from decisions

To have hold to save money

To have hold to decide what is preferred?

To have hold to nurture her own child

To have been active professionally

And still to have hold for home

This we all have without having women's empowerment

Actually, we are looking for awareness

To enlighten the power of Awesomeness

When will society will accept this?

Why WOMAN herself not looking for this?

To be arrogant and to earn is not a big deal

Our politeness and motherhood only can their mouth seal

It's too difficult to accept for this society

That the women are empowered from the day first in society

Why her strength is shown to her?

Why weakness always control her...

As a WOMAN let me tell you

Your emotions are your strength too

Don't be feminist to get power

Just be aware to use that power...

Don't run behind a petrichor

It can be everywhere, run for raining more

You are a flower don't run after fragrance

Don't let society proved that you don't have entrance...

It's time to understand the reality

The world is real, it's not the virtuality.

Prasanna K Kumar

I am Prasanna K Kumar from India. Being in social service I have written over 1000 macro and micro writes that mainly deals with philosophy, social concern and of course subtle romance. I own a blog under the name of nspk00786@blogspot.com. I have published more than 300 verses entitled *Dawn and Dusk*. I have also published above 500 poetic verses in Mirakee a poetry app. My writing does not come under conventional poetry category where meter, iambic structure, pentameter etc are mainstay, rather my penning assumes freestyle of its own rhythm. And my poetry also featured in FM radio of London. http://secklow1055.org/

THE KNOT

She felt like an angel
as he entranced her soul,
everything appeared
as a bed of roses, where
petals became mattress
to soothe her lithe body
as she laid on the couch
invisible thorns started
pricking her satin heart,
it was a startling moment
where she realised,
the nuptial knot was tied
by none other than a demon.

THE TEARS OF SOIL

The clouds gathered
with rumbling thunder,
the violent gush of winds
with eerie tunes engulfed
the clime, rained the bloody
pouring on the parched
land, the tears of soil
breached the surface
of earth, howls of vultures
pecking on corpses of life,
Gods prayed and demons
danced on the barren
burial grounds.

Sahaj Sabharwal

Sahaj Sabharwal loves writing poems and thoughts. He lives in Jammu city, Jammu and Kashmir, India. His date of birth is 17th March, 2002. He has been awarded many awards in poem writing at State level, National and international level. He was also selected to be invited for the INTERNATIONAL WRITERS MEETING IN TARIJA and HUNGARY, EUROPE. He was awarded with the INTERNATIONAL DIPLOMA IN WRITING and INTERNATIONAL MERIT CERTIFICATE IN WRITING and was PUBLISHED by THE YOUNG WRITERS ASSOCIATION IN UK and RECIEVED "CERTIFICATE OF PUBLICATION FROM UK." He was also awarded the 'India Star Proud Award' for his appreciable work and He is the author of the BOOK -: "Poems by Sahaj Sabharwal".

SMARTPHONE'S ADDICTION

What the hell!

Smartphone has made everyone enthral.

It is neither fake nor a lie,

Spectacles are seen on everyone\'s eye.

At shop, office, home or sitting alone,

No work done today in the absence of smart phone.

Youth, middle age or old,

Looks like they all watching mobile phones recklessly, with their brain sold.

Student's grades are getting low,

At last they just say Oh! No,

Holding their teacher's and parent's toe,

Ensuring that they will enhance, Just in flow.

Everyone has become Smartphone's addict,

After realization of time wasted on it,

Our mind says Oh! Shit.

On proper utilization of Smartphone,

We will definitely get a fully-fledged tree, with the seed which was sown.

INSULTING SIMPLE LIVING PEOPLE FOR JOYS

Today, the simple living people become prey of other people. In front of a huge crowd, these simple living people are being insulted. This is due to their calm and simple nature.

These simple living people are generally ignored and are being exploited by other people. They become a source of laughter for those people who get bored and want someone to entertain them.

First of all, the people who get bored, search for those people who are sitting idle or just ignored by someone or having simplicity in their life. Bored people just ask those people to come and sit with them and in front of their friends / relatives; they just make jokes of the simple people. The respect of the simple living people is just snatched by them and they play with the calm hearted people just like playing with useless toys. And the crowd surrounding the bored people also starts laughing on the calm hearted people by accompanying the bored people and insulting the simple living people without thinking about the feelings of those people having simple life and calm nature.

Reason: Only calm hearted and simple living people become the prey of those bored people because of their non-violent behaviour and their capability to dissolve the words spoken by them on simple living people. These calm hearted people don't get angry physically but internally their feelings get burned and being tolerant, they never show them or expel them off.

Conclusion: 1.) Calm hearted people should avoid being in contact of such bored people who are just making fun of them.

2.) They should make good friends and avoiding selfish friends.

3.) They should respect themselves more than anyone else.

4.) They should warn the bored people not to make fun of them or by complaining their parents/guardians or teachers.

5.) They should perform their activity carefully and with attention so that no one can make fun of them.

Mirza Saina Samreen

Mirza Saina Samreen is an inspired author and poetess.

She expresses her inspiration through her stories and poems.

Currently, she is pursuing BBA and aiming for her future Goals.

LIFE OF A WIDOW

Losing her husband, Just after a decade
Made the soul go insane!

Sitting in the room, Crying with deep pain
To get back her soul mate,
Who left the world at an early stage!

Days went on passing
But death of her husband yet caused distressing,
Becoming a widow was a most terrible thing
As she was living like a living corpse.

She relived again for the sake of her children,
As they were the only reason for her living
Playing the role of mother and father
She satisfied every need of her children.

Taking away all sympathies that surrounded her
She made her Children emphatically strong
Seeing her children smiling and enjoying

Made her relived the moments of her love again and again!

Without knowing where the future will lead

She hopefully waited for the best!!

GENDER DISCRIMINATION

Gender discrimination.

A controversial predicament,

Rising inequalities between men and women,

On issues like sex, health and education.

Biased in the fields of employment,

Killing the hopes of the innocent

Why can't a female be treated equally?

When nation has provided equality!

Stop Discriminating on the basis of Gender,

We are no one to judge the Abilities of others

Every person has equal rights

Make sure we treat them all equal.

Change the mindset of people

Nobody here is the losers

Everybody has equal right

Let them live their life.

Stop discrimination, start equality,

Injustice is gender inequality

Let's say, Gender equality a solution,

Gender equality a great freedom!

Sehrish Fuzel

Sehrish Fuzel is 20 and is currently pursuing her B.com (h) from Amity University, Gwalior. Besides writing, she loves sketching, listening to music and watching TV series. She also loves travelling and is a voracious reader. She believes that the true essence of poetry comes from the bottom of writer's heart which makes it the best medium to express emotions. You can connect with her at Instagram Handle: _. twinkiie. _/emaisehrishfuzel99@gmail.com

SHE

You only see what she shows,
unaware of the fact
that there is a lot more to know.
She hides her screams
beneath her laugh
She hides her pain and anguish
Beneath her smile.
You may represent her as weak
Through your bitter twisted lies,
You may try to oppress her
but unaffected by all.
She'll still rise...
Not realising her own worth
she carries the universe on her shoulders.
Not realising her strength,
she bears the power that is invincible.
Her beauty is reflected by her soul
and not by the figure which she carries.
Her strength is reflected
by the spark in her eyes

which is the gateway to her heart

Where love and compassion reside.

She is someone

who defines her own self

She is someone

Whose beauty never dies,

but with each passing moment it grows.

She is someone,

with a never-ending love

and in spite of brutality

it's the compassion that she shows.

Shruti Tayal

Shruti Tayal, daughter of Mr. Brijmohan Tayal and Mrs. Babita Tayal was brought up in Palwal, Haryana. She is 18 years old. Currently, she is pursuing her graduation in physics. She started writing almost two years ago to follow her instincts and now she traps her readers with her words. The purpose of her life is to make people realize their worth. She is a true example of determinant and hard working. She has worked in many anthologies as a co-author, promoter, and manager. Also, she has published her two anthologies named "Petals of Life" and "Eradication of Caste in Modern World" in which 60+ & 40 writers have been published respectively. Alongside, she is also the founder of "Spread Smile", a platform where she gives a nudge to all budding writers and helps them get published. Besides writing, she loves to read & review novels, cooking, etc. She wishes to be a novelist someday. You can connect with her via: Email: shrutitayal268@gmail.com

Instagram: @spread_smile_shruti_skye

Twitter: @shrutiskye

Facebook: https://www.facebook.com/shruti.tayal.1004

SURVIVOR WITH BROKEN WINGS

It's 3 am again,

Deep Silence, mistreated memories,

The situation has made me recollect all my sins,

And I act as nothing has happened to me,

Even my loneliness has left me,

I'm under a dark cloud,

Where society blames me

That I'm a trapped soul in freedom,

My mind gets troubled,

What's making things more painful?

Reassuring myself if I'm not the problem!

The pain has locked my body,

Voices whisper around me,

And the society blames that I'm a puzzled face,

My thoughts, my feelings, they never count

As I was never mattered for them,

From being bullied to being neglected

They call it a Drama,

In a fragile state of mind

I decide only to suicide,

But something pulls me back, wraps me in itself,

My inner self asks me, "Will society remember me?"

When I'll be gone, will they keep shut their shit?

The silence is even more deafening!

Sonali Sahu

Sonali Sahu, with PhD in English Literature, is a creative and ebullient face in the arena of creative writing, who exquisitely writes poetry and works as an editor of the magazine 'WAVES'. Her creative works are appreciated and followed by many of the literature lovers. She is a contributing writer and poet of 29 national and international anthologies. She is presently a PGT (English) in Mount Litera Zee School, Berhampur.

SHE IS NOT FOR SALE

The innocent soul as an angel

landed on this Earth

But no one understood her worth.

She became a common story of every home

Selling and buying a lady under God's dome.

Buyer wants a good mind, face and education

Seller has to give a huge treat hiding his pain and emotion.

Many are killed before they have a start.

All the feelings inside her filled get buried in her heart.

Why her colour and name matter to all

Many drops make sea not dew drops at all.

Whom to stop and whom to punish

We all are devils who bear these social evils.

Stand up girls! Raise your voice

Tell the world and its people

You are precious to be adorned

Not for sale.

Sonali Sharma

Sonali Sharma, a young girl from a small town, who wishes to achieve great heights and make her parents feel proud. She wishes to be a good and generous person. She's currently pursuing Bachelor's degree in Accounting and Finance, along with that she's pursuing ICWA. She's a great Book lover and passionate to write! One day, she wishes to be a known author.

POVERTY

You feel it deep,

How people; suffering it might feel

While undergoing such a phase.

Small children roaming around the street,

In search of food but a shine of hope in eyes.

No one wants to be in such a state,

People who are blessed still curse their fate.

Enjoying all the luxuries,

And just getting happy in a single bread.

Rich poverty is becoming a new trend.

The one seems struggle hard to reach,

While other on top, trying to pull down to street.

How can a nation develop?

When poverty in minds

Folds itself like an envelope!

Poverty prevails everywhere

One which is seen,

Other one blind folded.

The day blindfold gets unfold,

None will sleep down the street in cold.

WOMEN-OUT STANDS THE SOCIETY

The era "oh beti hui hai"

To this era "mari choriya choro se kam hai k"

Proved the worth of girl child!

People who felt offended then,

Seem regretting now!

Girls were never ever low as compared to boys,

The only thing, they were denied of rights

And were just treated like toys.

The dirt in the minds said it all.

For gaining the justice none was called.

After all a girl is as pure as Goddess,

And as bold as a warrior.

She's beyond any comparison,

Could you stand stiff bleeding,

Could be proud of your scars!

Girls are always equal,

Infact more than a man!

She unites the family and

Treats like her world.

How Could you commit a sin comparing her?

Sushil Kumar Gochhayat

Sushil Kumar Gochhayat is an eminent engineer rendering his services to National Aluminium Company Limited (A Government of India Enterprise), Damanjodi, Odisha, incumbent as Deputy Manager (Chemical). He is a logodaedalus and his penchant for writing has made him to produce many magnificent creations in literature that have been published in many popular magazines and anthologies proving his unparalleled excellence.

WOMAN

Acid couldn't deface

the surface of her strength,

bitter words couldn't

demotivate her,

hindrances couldn't

stop her path,

she stood with all vigour,

she fought with courage

to give condign punishment

to the culprits.

Never leaving the dream

to do something significant,

she never skived off work.

Maintaining the family,

filling the lacunae,

she never stopped,

she never stopped

believing one day

law will take its action

to destroy lawlessness

and brutality

and woman will remain

safe both inside and outside

of mother's womb.

World may not stand with her

Justice may come late,

But her hope will not diminish,

Her fight will never take back seat,

Her determination will never retreat,

Her determination will never retreat.

Tejaswi Vajinepalli

Tejaswi Vajinepalli is an avid reader and a passionate writer. He loves to express himself through his words. He is working in IT field and currently based in Chennai.

FROM THE SOCIETY AND INTO THE SOCIETY

I was a happy go merry guy leading a carefree life

Always admired but never adored eventually faced humiliation

Initially I laughed it off but the humiliation continued

I was pushed into extremities when criticism and isolation enveloped me.

I was deprived and endangered afraid of letting out my voice

Extrovert forced to be an introvert by the society

Alienated and judged just because my opinions were different

Fragile and shattered in fragments I lay.

She came in uninvited into my life from the same society that isolated me

Treated me like a normal person without any judgement

Made friends, listened out to me, cared for me with great concern

Showed me another part of society that I believed never existed.

She asked me to believe in myself and understand my worth
Never conceal your emotions within you, vent out
Cry out and it's absolutely okay for a man to cry
Made me realize that not everyone's opinion matter.

She came like an Angel sent by the Super Natural
Healed my soul and gave it the hope to live
Eradicated all my insecurities and worries,
Made me strong and a better individual in the same society.

A HABITUATED COMPROMISE

She tried to speak out,

His abuses stopped her.

She tried to express,

His attitude worried her.

She wanted him to feel,

His empathy is away from her.

She wished him to love,

His love is never with her.

She started to adjust,

He took the advantage.

She started to obey,

He took her to be for granted.

She tried and tried to give and get love,

Nevertheless, it remained a wish.

The person who was supposed to be her beloved

And the love of her life

Has now become a part of her daily routine

Who no longer treated her as a person?

Thondakur Rajkumar

Thondakur Rajkumar has born on April 04 2000. He is bilingual poet at English and Telugu. He has completed his SSC at zilla parshad high school, donkeshwar and Intermediate at Telangana state model school and junior college Nandipet. Now studying degree at girraj govt college Nizamabad. His poems published in monthly magazines, international poetry anthology and National anthology.

BIG BLUNDER OF ALMIGHTY GOD

Dear god!

I am a girl at my mother's womb,

Don't make my way to tomb.

I know you are an innocent,

But people do a comment.

If you boon them a girl child,

But they praised for a boy child.

They offered you garlands as bribe,

An innumerable vow with ascribe.

Why don't you alter mankind in them?

When you blossom Ruth in them.

God make my birth is mirth,

But why you do its false,

With my mother alive their else.

My family is with full of grieves,

By their thoughts without derives.

After day my way to rubbish bin,

Remember God your blunder again.

My solace else life begins to ends,

Between my mosquito friends.

SOLACE ELSE FROW LIFE.

Oh lord! Oh lord! Oh lord!

Please listen me oh God!

Why you have given this life,

Without anyone solace to life.

What blunder in vows I made?

Why grieve to me enigma bade?

You have offered my husband and son death,

Why doesn't offer me as same path.

With your doom displayed accident,

With your great righteousness moment.

Why you boon barren and widow curse,

Why don't boon as torture else corpse.

Oh God! Made me your way,

Please I don't want to be stay.

To see off propaganda phones,

They don't console my pains.

God please alter the man kind,

And blossom kind in the mind.

To survive the persons in difficulty,

And made this attitude eternity.

Tuheena Mohanty

Tuheena Mohanty, an introvert yet friendly young girl, currently pursuing her class 12th from ODM, Bhubaneswar. She is a strong believer of Karma. Doesn't intend to have a career in writing but somehow manages to express her feelings. She has been a part of many anthologies also been a compiler of DIVULGE- the potential to confess.

SHE

She's chubby,

she's skinny!

She's adorable,

she's vulnerable!

She's friends with males,

Blowing herself in the smoky flames!

She's sipping alcohol,

Hey guys! Look she's in camisole!

Her shorts are too hot,

Is she a slut?

She's helpless,

She's shameless!

She's aristaless,

She's abodeless!

She's goddess,

Yet a characterless!

Dear society,

Stop issues that include hateration,

Let it not continue up to more generations!

She may be

someone's daughter,

Someone's laughter!

Someone's wife,

Someone's life!

We all are not devils,

So, let's raise our voice against these social evils!